Dear mouse friends,
Welcome to the world of

Geronimo Stilton

THE RODENT'S GAZETTE
EDITORIAL STAFF

Geronimo Stilton
A learned and brainy
mouse; editor of
The Rodent's Gazette

Thea Stilton
Geronimo's sister and
special correspondent at
The Rodent's Gazette

Trap Stilton
An awful joker;
Geronimo's cousin and
owner of the store
Cheap Junk for Less

Benjamin Stilton
A sweet and loving
nine-year-old mouse;
Geronimo's favorite
nephew

Geronimo Stilton

THE TREASURE OF EASTER ISLAND

Scholastic Inc.

The publisher does not have any control over and does not assume any responsibility for author or third-party websites or their content.

Published by Scholastic Inc., 557 Broadway, New York, NY 10012. SCHOLASTIC and associated logos are trademarks and/or registered trademarks of Scholastic Inc.

ISBN 978-0-545-74614-4

Text by Geronimo Stilton
Original title *Il tesoro di Rapa Nui*
Cover by Giuseppe Ferrario (design) and Flavio Fausone (color)
Illustrations by Giuseppe Ferrario (design) and Flavio Fausone (color)
Graphics by Paolo Zadra

Special thanks to AnnMarie Anderson
Translated by Lidia Morson Tramontozzi
Interior design by Becky James

12 11 10 9 8 7 6 5 4 3 2 1   15 16 17 18 19/0

Printed in the U.S.A.   40
First printing 2015

An Adventure to Remember!

I'm ready to tell you about an incredible adventure I'll never forget. This story is very special to me because it takes place in·one of the most mysterious places on EARTH . . .

The whole thing started on a beautiful spring morning. Oops! What terrible manners! I haven't introduced myself yet. My name is Stilton, *Geronimo Stilton*, and I'm the publisher of *The Rodent's Gazette*, the most famouse newspaper on Mouse Island.

Anyway, that spring morning I was hard at work in my office. (For the record, I'm always hard at work when I'm in the office, even if my grandfather, William Shortpaws, says otherwise!) I was with Susie Shuttermouse, our new staff photographer. We were deciding which photo to put on the front page of our next issue. Susie is also best friends with my sister, Thea. And Thea is the newspaper's special correspondent.

Susie pointed to a photo of the Amazon

Susie Shuttermouse

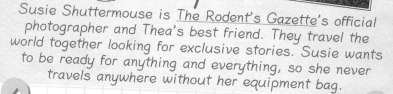

Susie Shuttermouse is <u>The Rodent's Gazette</u>'s official photographer and Thea's best friend. They travel the world together looking for exclusive stories. Susie wants to be ready for anything and everything, so she never travels anywhere without her equipment bag.

Susie's Equipment Bag

Susie's bag is enormouse! It has lots of hidden, zippered compartments. Each pocket holds a different item, such as a camera, pliers, scissors, energy bars, a toothbrush, etc. The bag also has many special features. It can become a backpack, a parachute, or an umbrella! And it's made of very lightweight but durable waterproof material.

rain forest. The image showed a crew of **rats** chopping down trees and vegetation.

"Listen to me, Geronimo," Susie squeaked. "You should put a story about the Amazon on the **front** page. We have to do something to keep these rats from **destroying** the rain forest! I risked my **fur** to take these photos. Now the least you can do is **PUBLISH** them!"

AMAZON RAIN FOREST - - - - - - - - - - - - →

"Nice work, Susie," I said proudly. "I can already see the **HEADLINE**: 'Amazon Rain Forest in Danger from —'"

Before I could finish, my office door *FLEW* open and my cousin Trap **BURST** in. He also works for the newspaper, though you'd never know it! He only shows up in the office when it's convenient for him. Anyway, he was pinching his nose with one paw, and he held an umbrella in his other paw.

A letter dangled by a string from the tip of the umbrella. And as if that wasn't weird enough, a cloud

Pee-yew!

5

of flies **buzzed** around the letter!

"You've got MAIL, Geronimo!" Trap squeaked. "And boy, does it **stink**!"

He snipped the string with a pair of scissors and the letter landed on my desk with a flutter.

"Yuck, yuck, yuck!" Trap screeched. "Rat-munching rattlesnakes, where's this thing from? A **garbage** dump? A sewage treatment plant? An underground cave full of **rancid roaches** that haven't bathed in years?"

He turned to leave, calling over his shoulder: "You'd better close the door before you open that thing, Cuz! Everyone in the newsroom is complaining about the awful **stench**!"

I sighed. Was it my fault someone had sent me the **stinkiest** piece of mail in all of

New Mouse City?!

A second later, Susie closed the door with a BANG!

Then she *dashed* to the window and threw it open. A GUST of wind blew into the office, making it much easier to breathe. ②

Next she took a pair of TWEEZERS out of her giant equipment bag. She carefully

Then she threw open the window. ②

Done!

Susie closed the door. ①

picked up the envelope. ③

Finally, she pulled out a **MAGNIFYING** glass and used it to examine the foul piece of mail. ④

"That's odd," Susie remarked. "This comes from **EASTER ISLAND**. Who would write to you from there, Geronimo?"

I shook my head in surprise.

"Musty muenster, I have no idea!" I

What a stench!

. . . and examined it carefully. ④

How odd!

She picked up the letter with a pair of tweezers . . . ③

exclaimed. "Easter Island is one of the most **MYSTERIOUS** places in the world . . . and it's in the middle of nowhere!"

My paws trembled with excitement as I opened that **strange**, stinky envelope. Another surprise awaited me inside . . . The letter was from my sister, THEA!

GERONIMO STILTON
THE RODENT'S GAZETTE
17 SWISS CHEESE CENTER
NEW MOUSE CITY, MOUSE ISLAND
13131

Dear Geronimo,

    I've found a map that leads to treasure on Easter Island, and I've decided to search for it! I'm on the island right now. But I'm afraid finding the treasure could be very difficult, so that's why I'm sending you a copy of the map. If you receive this letter before I'm able to call you, it's because I may be in danger and I need your help. Find me by following the directions on the map. See you soon!

Love,

THEA

P.S. Don't dillydally. Leave immediately!

P.P.S. Invite someone adventurous to come with you — someone like Wild Willie!

P.P.P.S. Take Susie with you as well. She can take photos to go along with my story, and The Rodent's Gazette will have the scoop of the year!

Furthermore: Remember to update your will before leaving. This island is very mysterious, and who knows what might happen on a search for treasure. You may be leaving your fur behind!

One Last Thing: I hope you didn't find this letter too stinky. I wanted to keep any sneaky rodents from opening it and reading the map, so I dipped this letter in guano (that's bird poop, in case you were wondering). It stinks so much no one would ever want to open it! Aren't you impressed with my ingenuity?

Find the biggest ahu and its fifteen protectors.
Turn west and search for the Great Water that is and isn't.
At the end of the day, follow the sun and you'll find the
Seven Young Explorers.
Take seven gigantic steps to the right, three warrior steps
to the left, and one baby step forward.
The Sigh of the Wind will take you far away to the
Big Black Bubble.
There, the sea hides an ancient secret . . .

THE TREASURE OF EASTER ISLAND!

TREASURE, TREASURE, TREASURE!

"**Wh-wh-what?**" I stammered. "A map? A treasure? Easter Island?"

My whiskers trembled with fear. I didn't want to go on a treasure hunt! In case you didn't know it, I'm a real scaredy-mouse.

As soon as I uttered the word treasure, the door flew open and smacked me in the snout.

"**OUCHIE!**" I squeaked.

It was my cousin Trap. He had clearly been standing just on the other side of the door, *eavesdropping*. He didn't even apologize.

"A treasure?" he squeaked, rubbing his paws together greedily. "I'm coming with you. Oh, what a beautiful word: treasure, treasure, treasure!"

"Trap, don't you understand?" I scolded him. "The treasure isn't important — Thea is! I received her letter, but she hasn't called. That means she's in **DANGER**!"

Susie tried to call Thea on the phone, but she **DIDN'T ANSWER** at home or on her cell phone.

1

2

3

4

"Rat-munching rattlesnakes!" I squeaked. "Thea must be in real **DANGER**! She always answers her cell phone."

I was so worried about my sister that I *fainted* from fear. As I said, I'm a real scaredy-mouse.

But Susie managed to revive me. First, she **smacked** my cheek. ① Then she pinched my ear. ② Next she poured **ICE-COLD** water from a vase of flowers over my snout. ③ Finally, she stuffed a piece of **cheese** into my mouth. ④

While I was trying to get myself together, Susie called Wild Willie. Do you

Wild Willie?

know him? He is an **ARCHAEOLOGIST** and a true adventure mouse!

"Wild Willie, is that you?" Susie squeaked. "It's Susie, the official photographer for *The Rodent's Gazette*. Thea has disappeared . . . There's a treasure map . . . Easter Island . . . **RIGHT**. We'll leave right away . . . **YEAH, YEAH** . . . Won't dillydally . . . **RIGHT, RIGHT, RIGHT**."

She hung up.

"Wild Willie is on his way," she squeaked with satisfaction. "We're leaving immediately."

"Wh-what do you mean?" I stammered. "We're leaving right now? But I have to **PACK** a bag! And turn on my **out-of-office** message! And say good-bye to my

Heeeelp!

sweet nephew Benjamin!"

Suddenly, a **GUST** of wind hit me right in the snout. Then I heard an **incredible** noise from outside my window.

Before I knew what was happening, a giant hook seemed to come out of the sky. A second later, I was dangling by my jacket collar as the hook **SCOOPED** me up and carried me away!

"Heeeelp!" I squeaked.

I **turned** toward Trap and Susie, hoping they'd pull me inside. But instead, Trap grabbed my tail, and Susie grabbed his.

"Go with the **adventure**!" Susie shouted with a giggle as the hook lifted the three of us into the air.

MOLDY MOZZARELLA! WHERE WERE WE GOING?!

I'M ALIVE!
I'M STILL ALIVE!

A midnight blue airplane with a fierce dragon painted on it flew overhead as we soared over the roofs of New Mouse City.

My whiskers quivered with fright. Have I mentioned that I get airsick? And that's when I'm actually **INSIDE** an airplane, not dangling below one!

"**HEEEEEEEEEEEEELP!**" I shrieked.

With a metallic screech, the cable above me began moving **UPWARD**. Finally, I landed inside the plane: **THUMP!**

"This is fabumouse!" Trap shouted.

"Awesome!" Susie squeaked in agreement.

But there were no shouts of excitement from me! I **kissed** the floor of the plane as I cried with relief.

"I'm alive! **I'm still alive!**"

"Well, for now..." a deep voice muttered. It was **Wild Willie**!

He was the one flying the plane! He handed me a map.

"Instead of wasting your breath, help me

figure out the route to Easter Island," he squeaked. "And then read this TRAVEL guidebook!"

I was about to protest, but he stared at me with his **PIERCING** eyes.

"Don't you want to find Thea?" Wild Willie asked. "Come on! Help me with the map. And don't make any mistakes, or we'll have to make an EMERGENCY landing in the middle of a stormy ocean or on top of a CRAGGY mountain peak . . ."

EMERGENCY LANDING?! I quickly agreed to help. But when I opened the map, what I saw gave me chills from the top of my head to the tip of my tail. Easter Island was FAR away and in the middle of NOWHERE! And when I read the travel guide, I realized there were many, many MYSTERIES surrounding the island . . .

Easter Island

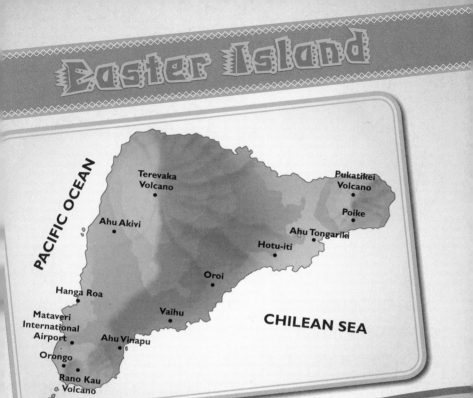

PACIFIC OCEAN

Terevaka Volcano

Ahu Akivi

Pukatikei Volcano

Poike

Ahu Tongariki

Hotu-iti

Oroi

Hanga Roa

Vaihu

CHILEAN SEA

Mataveri International Airport

Ahu Vinapu

Orongo

Rano Kau Volcano

This remote island is part of Chile. It lies more than two thousand miles west of South America and more than one thousand miles from its nearest island neighbor. The island was once home to the Rapa Nui people, who are famous for building incredible moai — volcanic rock statues that depict huge human heads. Easter Island has a mysterious charm that attracts many tourists.

That's Easter Island!

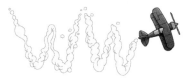

IS THAT IT? NO WAY!

We flew for hours and hours. Wild Willie kept his **GAZE** fixed on the flight **instruments**. He never moved away from the controls.

I, on the other paw, couldn't take my eyes off the foam-topped blue waves **churning**

Land!

and cRashing below us. The ocean seemed endless. According to my guidebook, the Polynesian people who had once explored the area navigated the ocean in simple outrigger CANOES! How terrifying!

Susie took photo after PHOTO.

"Does this plane do stunts?" she asked Wild Willie as she snapped a shot of him at the controls.

He raised his left eyebrow. "Obviously," he replied coolly.

"Pff! I doubt it," Trap muttered.

To prove himself, Wild Willie immediately leaned on the controls, sending the plane into a wild corkscrew.

"HEEEEELP!" I screeched.

"Is that it?" Trap scoffed. "No way! You can't do anything better?"

With a sudden lurch, the plane dove into

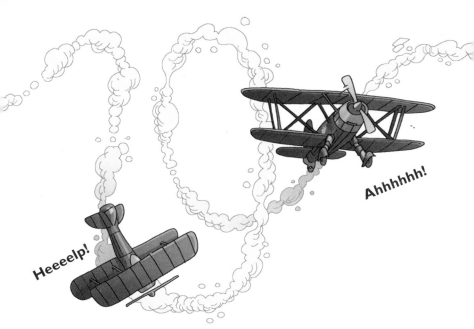

a death-defying spiral.

"Ahhhhhh!" I squeaked, terrified. "I don't want to lose my fur!"

"Oh, that's nothing," Trap teased Willie. "If I were behind the controls . . ."

Before Trap could finish his sentence, Wild Willie took the tiny plane through one breathtaking stunt after another.

During all these DAREDEVIL moves, I gripped the seat of the plane for dear life. My whiskers twisted with terror, and

Ugh! Ugh! Ugh!

I was so airsick I thought I might toss my cheese! Luckily, Susie's kindness saved me.

She rummaged through her equipment bag and found a bottle of bubbly seltzer water. "Here," she said. "This will help settle your stomach, Geronimo."

Thank goodmouse for her!

"Is that ENOUGH stunts, or do you want some more?" Wild Willie shouted to Trap over the ROAR of the plane's engine.

"Please tell him that's enough!" I begged

Trap. "I can't take another second of these loop-dee-loops!"

Trap scratched his snout and thought about it for what seemed like an eternity.

"Well, I have to admit those were some pretty **IMPRESSIVE** stunts," he conceded.

Only then did Wild Willie finally return the plane to a **HORIZONTAL** position. He grinned proudly.

A moment later, an island shaped like a **TRIANGLE** appeared on the horizon.

"We've arrived on Easter Island!" Susie squeaked excitedly.

"Yes, here we are, in the middle of NOWHERE," Wild Willie remarked **darkly**. "Did you remember to update your will, Geronimo?"

I shook my snout. When would I have had the TIME?

"Don't worry, Geronimo," Susie chirped. "I'll help you do it now. To whom would you like to leave *The Rodent's Gazette*?"

Trap TUGGED on my tail.

"Geronimo, my friend and favorite cousin," he said sweetly — a little TOO sweetly, if you ask me! "You're going to leave the paper to me, right? I know all about running a **newspaper**, unlike you. I think you should also leave me your antique cheese rind collection. And don't worry about your TOMBSTONE — I'll write something nice! How about: *Here lies Geronimo Stilton, a real scaredy-mouse! He met his end on Easter Island when he suffered an attack of uncontrollable fear.*"

That was something **nice**?!

"THAT'S ENOUGH!" I squeaked. "Why does everyone keep asking if I've updated my will, anyway?"

The **THREE** of them exchanged an understanding look. What were they keeping from me?

"He's a really *jittery* mouse, isn't he?" Wild Willie said.

"You're the ones who are making me jittery!" I said impatiently.

I put on my seat belt and closed my eyes. What kind of **DANGER** awaited me? My heart beat faster just thinking about it. But my desire to help Thea was stronger than any fear I felt. I opened my **WALLET** and took out a photo of my sister.

"I'll save you, little sister!" I whispered.

MY SISTER, THEA STILTON!

WELCOME TO RAPA NUI!

Before I knew it, the plane was landing at Mataveri International Airport. A friendly-looking rodent with golden fur and long **black** hair met us at the gate.

"Welcome to Rapa Nui!" she greeted us. "My name is Vaitea, and I will be your guide."

She presented each of us with a garland of **multicolored** flowers.

"We're not like other tourists," Trap boasted. I could tell he was trying to make a good *impression* on Vaitea. "We're here hunting for treas —"

Susie clapped her paw over Trap's snout before he could **finish**.

"Ahem, we're here on vacation, just like all these other tourists," Susie squeaked confidently. "We would love to see the island's most **iⁿteResTiⁿG** sights!"

Susie showed Vaitea a **PHOTO** of Thea. "This is our friend who was recently on

the island," she said. "Have you ever seen her?"

"No, I'm sorry," Vaitea replied, shaking her head. "She doesn't look familiar."

We were all hungry from our long flight, so Vaitea took us to a great restaurant in the harbor. We ate huge grilled shrimp, fish soup, and MAHI MAHI, a fish that is often served on the island. During dinner, Vaitea told us some of the history of Easter Island.

"Rapa Nui is the other name for Easter Island," she began. "It's also the name of the people who live here, and I'm proud

MAHI MAHI

Short Dictionary of the Rapanui Language

AHU: a structure or platform

HARE PA'ENGA: a traditional home that resembles an upside-down boat

'IORANA: hello or good-bye; a greeting

MATU'A: ancestor; father

MOAI: large statue

POKI: baby

RONGORONGO: wooden tablets with ancient carved writing

TOKI: tool used to carve stone

TOTORA: type of reed used to build rafts; a reed boat

VAI KAVA: ocean

Many inhabitants of Easter Island speak Rapanui, a Polynesian dialect. However, Chilean Spanish is the island's official language.

Rongorongo are ancient wooden tablets that feature carved symbols. These tablets have only been partially translated, so this written language is still a mystery!

to be one of them. My people speak two languages, Rapanui and Spanish."

Then she **taught** us a few words and phrases. I began taking notes: Rapanui was a very **interesting** language! At the end of dinner I showed off my knowledge and said to Vaitea: "*Māuru-uru!* (Thank you!)"

"*Rivariva!* (Very good!)" Vaitea replied, smiling. "Now, would you like to see a typical dance?" she asked. "A performance is about to begin!"

The lights **dimmed**. Many young rodents appeared on the stage and began to sing. The musicians played ukuleles and drums, and a few people began to dance.

Their movements **MiMiCKED** the daily activities of the Rapa Nui people, including swimming, fishing, and rowing a boat.

Then they danced a ritual dance showing warriors intimidating their enemies. Finally, they concluded with a dance in which a fishermouse and a maiden declared their love for each other. It was truly FABUMOUSE!

Susie snapped a lot of PHOTOS.

"We'll leave here with lots of very

INTERESTING material for *The Rodent's Gazette*. Thea will be very happy with my work!"

Hearing Thea's name brought me back to reality. We were here on a **MISSION**! Where was my sister, Thea? And was she in **DANGER**? We had to find out soon.

Look for the Biggest Ahu . . .

The next morning we gathered to decide what to do next. Wild Willie reread the RIDDLE on the map:

FIND THE BIGGEST AHU AND
ITS FIFTEEN PROTECTORS.
TURN WEST AND SEARCH FOR THE
GREAT WATER THAT IS AND ISN'T.
AT THE END OF THE DAY, FOLLOW
THE SUN AND YOU'LL FIND
THE SEVEN YOUNG EXPLORERS.
TAKE SEVEN GIGANTIC STEPS TO
THE RIGHT, THREE WARRIOR STEPS
TO THE LEFT, AND ONE BABY STEP
FORWARD.

THE SIGH OF THE WIND WILL
TAKE YOU FAR AWAY TO THE
BIG BLACK BUBBLE.
THERE, THE SEA HIDES
AN ANCIENT SECRET . . .
THE TREASURE OF
EASTER ISLAND!

"The first thing we need to do is to find an **AHU**," he concluded. "In fact, we need to find the biggest one on the island."

I checked my Easter Island GUIDEBOOK.

"The ahu are STONE platforms that were used as burial sites by the ancient inhabitants of Easter Island," I explained.

Hmm, let's see . . .

At that moment, Vaitea came in.

"Perfect timing!" Susie squeaked. "We were just talking about where we'd like to go **FiRST**. We'd like to see some of the island's **AHU**. Can you tell us which one is the **BIGGEST**?"

"That would be Ahu Tongariki," Vaitea replied with a smile. "It's one of the most

AHU TONGARIKI
Ahu Tongariki is the biggest ahu on Easter Island. The moai there face inland with their backs to the sea.

SPECTACULAR places on the island!"

When we got to Ahu Tongariki, the most MAJESTIC sight awaited us. The enormouse statues lined the shore, their backs to the ocean waves. Vaitea explained that the statues — called moai — were built to guard and **PROTECT** the island.

"Get your CAMERA ready, Susie!"

They're amazing!

Trap shouted as he ran toward a moai. "I'm going to climb to the top."

"**STOP!**" Vaitea squeaked in dismay. "You can't climb a moai! Please, you shouldn't even touch it! This is my **ancestors'** sacred burial ground."

Susie grabbed Trap by the **TAiL** a second before he began to climb.

"What do you think you're doing?!" she scolded him.

During this whole mess, I was busy counting the moai on the stone platforms.

"One, two, three, four, five . . . thirteen, fourteen, **FiFteen**!" I counted. "These are the fifteen protectors the riddle talks about. We figured out the first **CLUE**!"

"Now we have to turn west and find the **Great Water**," whispered Wild Willie. "But I don't understand why it 'is and isn't.' What do you think that means?"

SEARCHING FOR THE GREAT WATER

We headed west with Vaitea, but we didn't see even a drop of water anywhere!

"Is there any water on EASTER ISLAND?" Susie asked her. "I haven't seen any so far."

"Well, there is and isn't much water on the island," Vaitea replied mysteriously. "There are three crater lakes. But during the dry season, there isn't much water in them. During the RAINY season, though, it's another story . . ."

My tail twisted with excitement. Vaitea had referred to water that "is and isn't"!

"Is one of these crater lakes near here?" I asked eagerly.

She nodded and motioned for us to follow

her up a STEEP path. We turned a corner, and there before us was a rocky **crater** etched deep into the ground.

"This is where the Great Water flows . . . when there is any!"

This is where the Great Water flows?

SEVEN YOUNG EXPLORERS

Wild Willie smiled with satisfaction and immediately checked the MAP.

"The map says, 'At the end of the day, follow the sun,'" he said. "So we should head west, since that's where the sun sets."

I scratched my SNOUT.

"Yes, but what are the Seven Young Explorers?"

We got back in Vaitea's SUV and headed toward the western shore of the island. As we mused over the riddle, we were as quiet as mice.

Night had already fallen, and Vaitea stared at the dark sky. A silvery moon shone brightly.

"In the olden days, it was precisely on **NIGHTS** like these that our ancestors performed **SACRED** ceremonies near the moai by the sea," she told us. "Those ceremonies recalled the ancient traditions of Polynesia, which is where my courageous **forefathers** came from when they explored this new land."

It all sounded very, very **familiar**. But where had I heard it **before**?

Vaitea's words kept turning over and over in my head. Then suddenly it was like a **light bulb**

Moai by the sea . . .

Polynesia . . .

forefathers explored . . .

Ancient traditions . . .

Sacred ceremonies . . .

went off. I had read those words before in my travel guide! I leafed through it until I found what I was looking for.

"Listen to this!" I told the others, reading from the book. "'Most of the moai on Easter Island look inward with their backs to the sea. But there is one group of **seven** moai that look toward the sea.'" I turned toward Vaitea eagerly. "Do you know where these seven moai are?"

Listen to this!

"Of course," she replied immediately. "They are at **AHU AKIVI**. I can take you there right now if you wish. They represent the seven young explorers who left Polynesia to look for new land, and finally reached **EASTER ISLAND**."

Susie, Trap, Wild Willie, and I exchanged a look. We had solved the next **CLUE**!

Vaitea turned the SUV onto a long dirt road full of potholes. Then we came to a **STOP** in a clearing. We quickly climbed out, eager with **excitement**. The four of us ran toward the summit of the small hill. At the top of the hill was a **platform** with seven moai standing in a row. The full moon bathed them with a silvery light, surrounding them with a halo of **mystery**.

"These must be the Seven Young Explorers!" I whispered to Susie.

AHU AKIVI

Ahu Akivi is found inland instead of along the coast like the other ahu on Easter Island. It is also the only site where the moai look out toward the ocean.

THE SIGH OF THE WIND

Vaitea noticed me and Susie whispering, and she studied us closely with her BRIGHT eyes.

"Excuse me, I don't mean to be rude, but I don't think you've told me the truth about why you are here," she began. "I have a feeling you're not simply TOURISTS."

I looked at my friends. I was more than happy to tell Vaitea the truth, but I wasn't sure what they were thinking.

Susie smiled. "It's okay with me if we tell her," she said. "I TRUST Vaitea."

Wild Willie nodded. "Me, too."

"Hmpf!" Trap squeaked. "Well, I don't want to tell her. I don't want to share the treasure with anyone!"

Susie gave Trap a **STERN** look.

"Aren't you ashamed of being so **greedy**?" she asked. "We're searching for Thea, not the treasure!"

"*You* might be searching for Thea, but *I'm* looking for the treasure," Trap admitted with a shrug. He didn't seem **ashamed** at all!

The two of them began squabBling. Wild Willie had to pull them apart!

"Three to one," Willie told Trap. "The **majority** wins. Geronimo, explain everything to Vaitea!"

"My sister, Thea, came here in search of a treasure, but she's gone missing!" I told Vaitea. "She never returned home to New Mouse City. So now we're looking for the same treasure in the hope of finding her!"

Vaitea thought it over.

"I'll help!" she offered.

Seven gigantic steps to the right . . .

Three warrior steps to the left . . .

Meanwhile, Trap was busy following the **directions** on the map. He had run in front of the seven moai and began counting in a **LOUD** voice.

"Okay," he squeaked. "The map says to take seven gigantic steps to the right, three warrior steps to the left, and one **baby** step forward . . ."

He had just taken the baby step when his paw landed on something that looked like a plain old rock. But it wasn't a rock. It was a HOLE!

One baby step forward . . .

Help!

With a yelp, Trap fell into it — **DOWN**, **DOWN**, **DOWN**!

We ran toward the HOLE, but it was too late. My cousin had disappeared!

Wild Willie TWIRLED his whiskers thoughtfully.

"The riddle did say, 'The Sigh of the Wind will take you far away,'" he said.

"We've got to do something!" Susie squeaked.

"Are you ready for an ADVENTURE?" Wild Willie shouted. "If you are, follow me!"

He held out his 🐾🐾🐾 to Susie, who held out her paw to me. In turn, I held out my paw to Vaitea. A moment later, Wild Willie JUMPED into the hole, taking the rest of us with him!

MOLDY MOZZARELLA! How do I get myself into these messes?!

THE BIG BLACK BUBBLE

We found ourselves inside a damp, **dark** underground tunnel. I was terrified! I couldn't see a whisker!

What's more, there was a continuous rustling noise, as if a **GIGANTIC** creature was lying there, breathing in the dark. I let out a shriek of terror as we plummeted

deeper and **deeper** into the underground passageway. We seemed to be traveling to the center of the **EARTH**. A moment later, I was no longer sliding down the tunnel — I was floating in the air! The Sigh of the Wind was carrying us along!

We floated along in the tunnel for a long time. Then instead of descending farther, we began to rise until the wind finally deposited us on **FIRM** ground. Trap had already emerged and was rubbing his

BRUISED tail. Wild Willie bounded out, but his hat remained floating in midair as if on top of an invisible fountain. Willie grabbed it quickly and put it back on his head.

I glanced around me and made sure everyone was okay.

"Trap, Susie, Wild Willie, Vaitea, and me!" I squeaked. "All here!"

I breathed a sigh of relief. Then I looked around, taking in my surroundings.

We found ourselves inside an enormouse cave with a **rounded** ceiling. It looked like a big, **DARK** bubble. There was a saltwater lagoon in the middle of the cave. I gently touched the wall: It was dark, porous volcanic rock.

"The **Big Black Bubble**!" whispered Susie. "We found it!"

"This is where the treasure is!" Trap squeaked with excitement.

Susie turned to him, an ANGRY look on her snout.

"No, this is where we might find Thea!" she corrected him. "How can you only think of the treasure? You should be ashamed of yourself!"

Meanwhile, Wild Willie examined the map.

"I checked our direction with the compass while we were traveling on the Sigh of the Wind," he whispered. "We traveled underground in a SOUTHWEST direction."

"That means we're now right under the Rano Kau CRATER!" Vaitea added. "We're in the heart of a volcano. And this must be a secret underground lagoon.

I've never seen it on any map, and I've been a guide on this island since I was a tiny mouselet!"

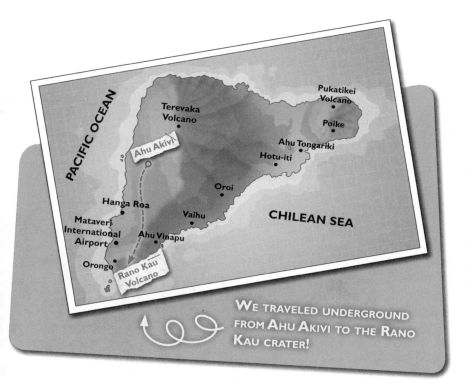

WE TRAVELED UNDERGROUND FROM AHU AKIVI TO THE RANO KAU CRATER!

PIRATES IN THE NIGHT

As they were talking, Susie snapped some photos of Wild Willie checking the map. The camera's flash lit the rocks behind us.

At the same time, Trap sneezed. The sound bounced off the surrounding walls, ECHOING loudly.

ACHOO! Choo! Choo! Choo!

A second later we heard a squeak. We weren't **alone** in the cave! And the flash of the camera and the echo of the sneeze had revealed our presence to whoever else was there.

Wild Willie motioned to us to keep **quiet**. Then he **SCAMPERED** behind some rocks and squatted down. We immediately followed his example. A moment later, we heard an **unfriendly** voice.

"Search there, at the end of the cave," the voice commanded. "And if you find anyone, bring them to me!"

"Maybe somebody came looking for that **nosy** little mouse and the professor," another voice replied.

I shivered. Was "that nosy mouse" my **SISTER**, Thea? But who was the professor?

"Let's get back to the **SHIP**!" the first voice yelled. "We have to finish loading the treasure. We'll leave **TONIGHT**!"

Uh-oh!

I'm scared!

"Yes, Captain," the other
rodent replied. "But what are
we going do with our prisoners? They
know **EVERYTHING**. We can't leave
them here!"

My whiskers trembled with fear.

"I'll figure it out later," grumbled the
captain. "Now let's go! Get the **PRISONERS**

Let's get back
to the ship!

Yes, Captain!

and bring them to the ship. They may still be useful!"

Someone was coming toward us, but Wild Willie signaled to us to follow him quietly. Afraid of being seen, we slithered across the cave floor on our elbows until we reached the shore of the lagoon, where we saw a giant PIRATE SHIP!

The ship had a SLIM shape and a huge sail to better cruise the waves. It was completely black — including the sails — and I could see its name on the side: PHANTOM OF THE NiGHT.

Susie pointed to something hanging from the TIP of a rock, high above us. It was a giant cage! Inside was my sister, Thea, and Professor Von Dustyfur, a famouse ARCHAEOLOGIST who specializes in ancient treasures.

The short, ROUND pirate moved toward the cage. I was about to RUN over to save my sister and the professor when Wild Willie grabbed me by the tail.

"Wait!" he whispered. "Just be quiet. Let's see what happens."

The pirate lowered the CAGE using a pulley. Then he opened it, nudged my sister and the professor out of the cage, and TIED their paws behind their backs. He left them behind a giant pile of CRATES.

"Don't move, got

Argh!

Prisoners, come to me!

it?" he hissed. "The captain hasn't decided what to do with you yet!"

The other **PIRATES** loaded the crates onto the ship one at a time, arranging them neatly in the cargo compartment. As the pirates worked, the captain *BARKED* insults at his crew.

"Hurry up or I'll feed you to the **SHARKS**

for dinner!" he squeaked **menacingly**.

Soon all the pirates had disappeared inside the ship, leaving Thea and the professor **alone**. I signaled to the others, and we crept quickly but quietly to their side.

"**Shhh!**" Thea, it's me, Geronimo!" I whispered. "We came to **save** you!"

THE TREASURE OF RAPA NUI

Thea's eyes LIT UP when she saw me. Luckily, she and the professor remained **silent**. I picked up a **SHARP** sliver of rock and used it to saw through the ropes that bound their paws.

"Follow me," I whispered to them. "But don't make a sound!"

The pirates were busy preparing for their

departure, so they didn't see us *sneak* away from the ship. We slipped behind some rocks out of the pirates' view.

"Thank you, Geronimo!" Thea said, **hugging** me affectionately. "I knew you'd come save me!"

Professor Von Dustyfur also thanked me *warmly*. I introduced Susie, Trap, Wild Willie, and Vaitea.

"I would never have been able to find you without their **help**," I told Thea and the professor.

"What are these **PIRATES** up to?" Willie asked, pointing to the ship.

"Well, I came to the island and followed the instructions on the map, just like you," Thea explained. "First I found the largest **AHU** with the fifteen moai, then the Great Water, then the Seven Young Explorers, and

1 Thea arrived on Easter Island and searched for the precious treasure by following the directions on the map.

2 She entered the Tunnel of the Sigh of the Wind . . .

3 She came to the Big Black Bubble . . .

4 . . . and she was captured by pirates! That's when she met the professor, who had been their prisoner for man months.

finally the Big Black Bubble."

The rest of us leaned in, eager to hear what happened **next**.

"Here, under the Big Black Bubble, I found the real treasure of Rapa Nui. But unfortunately, I also found these pirates, and I was **CAPTURED**. That's when I met the professor. He was the pirates' **HOSTAGE**!"

The professor sighed. "It's true," he explained. "They forced me to unearth many ancient treasures for them."

"Bingo!" Trap squeaked with excitement. "Tell us about the treasure of Rapa Nui. Is it a chest of GOLD coins? Or a heap of **PRECIOUS** stones and pearls?"

Susie elbowed him sharply.

But Thea knew our cousin Trap too well. She just smiled at him.

"Cousin, the treasure I found in this cave is very *precious*, but you won't be taking it home to New Mouse Island with you," she said simply. "This treasure is for the inhabitants of Easter Island!"

"But **WHAT** is it?" Trap squeaked.

Thea pointed to seven canoes woven from reeds. They had been **hidden** in a corner

of the cave.

"**What are those?**" Trap asked.

"This is the treasure of Rapa Nui!" Thea said, gesturing to the seven small boats. "These are the **seven** ancient canoes that the **seven** courageous young explorers used to travel to Easter Island from Polynesia," she explained.

"OOOOHH... THAT'S iT?"

Trap moaned, his whiskers drooping with disappointment.

"Yes," Thea said with a smile. "I was searching for the seven ancient canoes. But the PIRATES were looking for another treasure — one they found by forcing the professor to help them! Now they're loading it onto their ship ... Come on, I'll show you!"

We followed Thea to a huge block covered

with a cloth on the shore of the lagoon.

"This treasure was found at the bottom of the sea," Thea whispered.

She lifted a corner of the cloth to reveal a bright, shining surface. It was a moai made of solid GOLD!

"Now, this is what I call a treasure!" Trap squeaked, licking his whiskers greedily. "Let's see now. I only need a teeny-tiny piece of this statue and I'll be RICH! Why don't

Come and look!

Wow!

I just chip off a little sliver . . ."

Susie **pinched** his ear.

"Don't you dare touch it!" she warned.

Wild Willie looked at him sternly.

"The moai are SACRED here in Rapa Nui," he said seriously. "Those pirates will soon regret taking a treasure that does not belong to them."

"Okay, okay." Trap sulked. "I was only kidding!"

I only need a teeny-tiny piece . . .

Don't you dare!

THE SEVEN CANOES

We barely had time to cover up the treasure again before we heard the captain bark, "**LOAD THE MOAI!**" to the pirates.

A giant crane descended from the ship's deck, grabbing the gold moai and lifting it up onto the ship.

Thea desperately turned to Wild Willie. "**What can we do?**" she asked.

"We have to take **ACTION**!" he replied. "Let's get out of here, **FAST**, and look for help!"

Vaitea turned toward the **tunnel** we had entered from.

"We can't leave that way," she said. "The wind only blows in this **direction**!"

Wild Willie smiled.

"We'll leave by sea . . . in the **SEVEN CANOES**!"

Luckily, the **cool** temperature in the

Follow me!

tunnel had preserved the canoes over time. They were in *perfect* condition, and very fast! We began to paddle, careful not to make a sound.

As we got closer and closer to the ship, I was so scared the pirates might see us. My whiskers **trembled** with fright! **Luckily**, the pirates were too busy moving the moai. They didn't notice us slip by silently in the DARK water. We paddled around the ship and headed to the mouth of the cave. When we finally emerged onto the open sea, we found ourselves under a starry **NIGHT** sky that was lit up by the silvery LIGHT of the moon.

We saw a small beach nearby. Wild Willie was first to set his paw on **land**.

"Let's quickly gather some **dry** wood," he said. "We'll light a big **FIRE** and then I'll make some **signals** that will attract the attention of mice all the way in the village!" While we threw more WOOD on the fire, Wild Willie used a blanket to create **smoke** signals. He used

They'll see our signals!

Here's some more wood!

Morse code to send a distress signal: **SOS**.

Suddenly, we saw the bow of the **PHANTOM OF THE NIGHT** emerge from the secret cave. The pirates' ship was weighed down heavily with the **GOLD** moai. Unfortunately for us, they spotted our fire right away. The pirates pointed their **cannons** in our direction, and we could hear the captain issue his command.

"**Shoot** those spies!" the captain growled. "Ready! Aim! Fire!"

"Help!" I **SQUEAKED**. "They'll flatten

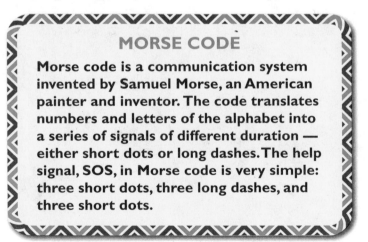

MORSE CODE

Morse code is a communication system invented by Samuel Morse, an American painter and inventor. The code translates numbers and letters of the alphabet into a series of signals of different duration — either short dots or long dashes. The help signal, SOS, in Morse code is very simple: three short dots, three long dashes, and three short dots.

us into mouse pancakes!"

I closed my eyes and waited for the cannonball to **Squash** us, but nothing happened! I slowly opened one eye and then the other, and saw why. The pirates' ship was **Sinking** from the weight of the gold moai!

Wild Willie chuckled.

"I knew those pirates would be sorry they **stole** that!" he said.

A moment later, a helicopter appeared in the **NIGHT** sky, dozens of boats sailed over the horizon and headed toward our beach, and cars and trucks **SPED** toward us over land. Everyone had seen our **SOS** and had come to our aid!

And as for the pirates who had been **shipwrecked** in the middle of the bay — well, they wouldn't be getting away.

GOOD-BYE!

We gave the seven canoes to the inhabitants of Easter Island. They were so happy to be reunited with such a precious historical treasure — one that had led to the discovery of Rapa Nui!

To thank us, they organized an amazing

PARTY for us on the beach. They sang and danced for us and put flower garlands around our necks.

"What will you do about the GOLD moai?" Trap asked Vaitea during the party. "Are you going to fish it out of the water?"

Vaitea shook her head.

"It's resting in the sea again," she replied. "And that's where it's going to stay!"

Soon it was time for us to say good-bye.

We climbed into Vaitea's SUV and headed
to the airport, the sounds of the Polynesian
music and the blue sea fading behind us.

"Thank you for returning the treasure to
the Rapa Nui people," Vaitea told us.

"No, thank you!" I replied. "We couldn't
have done it without your **HELP**!"

We waved good-bye as we boarded Wild
Willie's *plane*.

Wild Willie settled into his pilot's seat.

"Captain here," he said to himself with
a smile. "We're leaving Easter Island. In a
few hours we'll be flying over the coast of
CHILE. Our trip will continue all the
way home to Mouse Island!"

Suddenly, I realized that our **incredible**
adventure had come to an end. We were
going home!

I thought of all my **friends** waiting for

me and for Thea back in New Mouse City. I was especially looking forward to seeing my adorable nephew Benjamin. As I thought of my loved ones on Mouse Island, I looked out the window of the plane. The triangular outline of Easter Island, which was wrapped in a mass of clouds, receded in the distance.

"Good-bye, Rapa Nui!" I whispered softly under my whiskers.

Good-bye, Rapa Nui!

SPECIAL EDITION OF *THE RODENT'S GAZETTE*!

As soon as we landed at New Mouse City's airport, I hurried to the office of *The Rodent's Gazette*.

"Hello!" I greeted the staff. "I'm back from Easter Island, and I need everyone's help to put out an **EXTRA-SPECIAL** edition of the paper!"

The entire staff pitched in, and in just a few hours, we had put together an amazing special edition of *The Rodent's Gazette*. It included notes from Thea's diary and Susie's **incredible** photographs. That evening, the paper went **ON SALE**.

IT WAS A FABUMOUSE SUCCESS!

THE RODENT'S GAZETTE

The most famouse newspaper on Mouse Island

THE TREASURE OF EASTER ISLAND: FOUND!

NEW MOUSE CITY— Special correspondent Thea Stilton of *The Rodent's Gazette* and Professor Von Dustyfur, the noted archaeologist and expert in ancient treasures, have returned home to Mouse Island after being abducted by

pirates. The famouse journalist had gone to Easter Island in search of a lost treasure. There, she was captured by a band of ruthless pirates who had been holding Professor Von Dustyfur captive . . . (*continued*)

SUSIE SHUTTERMOUSE'S PHOTOGRAPHS

Trap stuffing
his snout
with shrimp

Geronimo encounters
a mysterious moai

The joy of dance!

Don't touch the moai, Trap!

Thea and the professor: the pirates' prisoners

Geronimo about to toss his cheese

The seven canoes: the real treasure of Rapa Nui!

Everyone had worked so hard on the newspaper, and I was hoping my grandfather, **William Shortpaws**, would be pleased. But all he did was pinch my **ear**.

"I have to admit that this time you did a pretty good job, Grandson," he barked. "But don't get **comfortable**! I've got my eye on you all the time, got it?"

I just rolled my eyes at him.

Night fell and I headed *home* at last. As I walked down the streets of New Mouse City, I met rodents around every **CORNER**.

They greeted me with **hugs** and smiles and asked me lots of questions about my adventure.

"It's nice to have you back here in New Mouse City. We missed you!"

I was so happy to be surrounded by so many **FRIENDS** and neighbors who loved me.

FINALLY HOME . . .
OR MAYBE NOT?

I finally arrived home, feeling exhausted. With a *sigh* of relief I put on my pajamas, made myself a nice cup of *hot* tea, and slipped beneath the covers of my *comfy* bed. It felt so good to be back!

Then the telephone *rang*.

"Hello?" I answered. "Stilton here. Geronimo Stilton!"

I heard Susie's familiar squeak.

"Hi, Geronimo!" she chirped brightly. "I really liked traveling with you."

Then I heard Thea's voice in the background.

"Tell him he's coming with us on our next trip!" she squeaked.

"That's right," Susie said. "We have another MYSTERY to solve — and we're going to Machu Picchu in PERU!"

Are you ready for an adventure?

"Don't worry, Cuz, I'm coming, too!" shouted Trap. I guess he was also there. "Aren't you **thrilled**? Now pack your little things and we'll come by to pick you up soon!"

"That's right, Cheesehead!" Wild Willie chimed in. "Get ready for an adventure!"

"**N-no!**" I stammered. "That is, thanks a million, but I'm not ReaDY. I mean, I'd love to come, but I have too much **work** to catch up on. So, **no, thanks**! Have a nice trip. *Good-bye!*"

I heard a chorus of confused protests at the other end of the phone. But then Wild Willie's deep voice cut them off.

"If we say YOU'RE coming, YOU'RE coming," he squeaked. "Period!"

"Got it, Cuz?" Trap shouted. "Period! That means **no excuses**!"

"You'll see, Geronimo!" Thea added. "You're actually very ready for the next adventure!"

"No, no, no!" I replied. "I'm telling you I'm not ready at all!"

But unfortunately they had already hung up the phone.

I stayed in bed and thought about it for a while as my whiskers quivered with uncertainty. But then my eyes fell on a PHOTO of the five of us on Easter Island. I looked happy in it, and I hate to admit it, but . . . I almost looked like an adventurous mouse! I sighed and looked out the WINDOW

to the landscape of New Mouse City.

It was a familiar view, and one that I knew well: There was SINGING STONE SQUARE, and the **Fashion Center**, and the harbor with its bobbing sailboats . . .

Yes, it was great being home. But it had also been great going on an amazing adventure far, far away. When you're traveling, everything is a challenge and courage is greatly rewarded. I stared far off into the horizon. Suddenly I felt BRAVE and confident.

"I am ready for a new adventure!" I exclaimed. "A **whisker-licking**-good one!"

And I promise to tell you all about it in my next BOOK. Rodent's honor!

Ah, sweet New Mouse City!

Be sure to read all my fabumouse adventures!

#1 Lost Treasure of the Emerald Eye

#2 The Curse of the Cheese Pyramid

#3 Cat and Mouse in a Haunted House

#4 I'm Too Fond of My Fur!

#5 Four Mice Deep in the Jungle

#6 Paws Off, Cheddarface!

#7 Red Pizzas for a Blue Count

#8 Attack of the Bandit Cats

#9 A Fabumouse Vacation for Geronimo

#10 All Because of a Cup of Coffee

#11 It's Halloween, You 'Fraidy Mouse!

#12 Merry Christmas, Geronimo!

#13 The Phantom of the Subway

#14 The Temple of the Ruby of Fire

#15 The Mona Mousa Code

#16 A Cheese-Colored Camper

#17 Watch Your Whiskers, Stilton!

#18 Shipwreck on the Pirate Islands

#19 My Name Is Stilton, Geronimo Stilton

#20 Surf's Up, Geronimo!

#21 The Wild, Wild West

#22 The Secret of Cacklefur Castle

A Christmas Tale

#23 Valentine's Day Disaster

#24 Field Trip to Niagara Falls

#25 The Search for Sunken Treasure

#26 The Mummy with No Name

#27 The Christmas Toy Factory

#28 Wedding Crasher

#29 Down and Out Down Under

#30 The Mouse Island Marathon

#31 The Mysterious Cheese Thief

Christmas Catastrophe

#32 Valley of the Giant Skeletons

#33 Geronimo and the Gold Medal Mystery

#34 Geronimo Stilton, Secret Agent

#35 A Very Merry Christmas

#36 Geronimo's Valentine

#37 The Race Across America

#38 A Fabumouse School Adventure

#39 Singing Sensation

#40 The Karate Mouse

#41 Mighty Mount Kilimanjaro

#42 The Peculiar Pumpkin Thief

#43 I'm Not a Supermouse!

#44 The Giant Diamond Robbery

#45 Save the White Whale!

#46 The Haunted Castle

#47 Run for the Hills, Geronimo!

#48 The Mystery in Venice

#49 The Way of the Samurai

#50 This Hotel Is Haunted!

#51 The Enormouse Pearl Heist

#52 Mouse in Space!

#53 Rumble in the Jungle

#54 Get into Gear, Stilton!

#55 The Golden Statue Plot

#56 Flight of the Red Bandit

Special Edition!

The Hunt for the Golden Book

#57 The Stinky Cheese Vacation

#58 The Super Chef Contest

#59 Welcome to Moldy Manor

Special Edition!

The Hunt for the Curious Cheese

#60 The Treasure of Easter Island

Up next!

#61 Mouse House Hunter

Join me and my friends as we travel through time in these very special editions!

THE JOURNEY THROUGH TIME

BACK IN TIME:
THE SECOND JOURNEY THROUGH TIME

Don't miss any of these exciting Thea Sisters adventures!

Thea Stilton and the
Dragon's Code

Thea Stilton and the
Mountain of Fire

Thea Stilton and the
Ghost of the Shipwreck

Thea Stilton and the
Secret City

Thea Stilton and the
Mystery in Paris

Thea Stilton and the
Cherry Blossom Adventure

Thea Stilton and the
Star Castaways

Thea Stilton: Big Trouble
in the Big Apple

Thea Stilton and the
Ice Treasure

Thea Stilton and the
Secret of the Old Castle

Thea Stilton and the
Blue Scarab Hunt

Thea Stilton and the
Prince's Emerald

Thea Stilton and the Mystery
on the Orient Express

Thea Stilton and the
Dancing Shadows

Thea Stilton and the
Legend of the Fire Flowers

Thea Stilton and the
Spanish Dance Mission

Thea Stilton and the
Journey to the Lion's Den

Thea Stilton and the
Great Tulip Heist

Thea Stilton and the
Chocolate Sabotage

Thea Stilton and the
Missing Myth

Thea Stilton and the
Lost Letters

Thea Stilton and the
Tropical Treasure

Be sure to read all of our magical special edition adventures!

THE KINGDOM OF FANTASY

THE QUEST FOR PARADISE:
THE RETURN TO THE KINGDOM OF FANTASY

THE AMAZING VOYAGE:
THE THIRD ADVENTURE IN THE KINGDOM OF FANTASY

THE DRAGON PROPHECY:
THE FOURTH ADVENTURE IN THE KINGDOM OF FANTASY

THE VOLCANO OF FIRE:
THE FIFTH ADVENTURE IN THE KINGDOM OF FANTASY

THE SEARCH FOR TREASURE:
THE SIXTH ADVENTURE IN THE KINGDOM OF FANTASY

THE ENCHANTED CHARMS:
THE SEVENTH ADVENTURE IN THE KINGDOM OF FANTASY

THE PHOENIX OF DESTINY:
AN EPIC KINGDOM OF FANTASY ADVENTURE

THEA STILTON: THE JOURNEY TO ATLANTIS

THEA STILTON: THE SECRET OF THE FAIRIES

THEA STILTON: THE SECRET OF THE SNOW

THEA STILTON: THE CLOUD CASTLE

MEET
GERONIMO STILTONIX

He is a spacemouse — the Geronimo Stilton of a parallel universe! He is captain of the spaceship *MouseStar 1*. While flying through the cosmos, he visits distant planets and meets crazy aliens. His adventures are out of this world!

#1 Alien Escape

#2 You're Mine, Captain!

#3 Ice Planet Adventure

#4 The Galactic Goal

#5 Rescue Rebellion

Meet
GERONIMO STILTONOOT

He is a cavemouse — Geronimo Stilton's ancient ancestor! He runs the stone newspaper in the prehistoric village of Old Mouse City. From dealing with dinosaurs to dodging meteorites, his life in the Stone Age is full of adventure!

#1 The Stone of Fire

#2 Watch Your Tail!

#3 Help, I'm in Hot Lava!

#4 The Fast and the Frozen

#5 The Great Mouse Race

#6 Don't Wake the Dinosaur!

#7 I'm a Scaredy-Mouse!

#8 Surfing for Secrets

#9 Get the Scoop, Geronimo!

ABOUT THE AUTHOR

 Born in New Mouse City, Mouse Island, **GERONIMO STILTON** is Rattus Emeritus of Mousomorphic Literature and of Neo-Ratonic Comparative Philosophy. For the past twenty years, he has been running *The Rodent's Gazette*, New Mouse City's most widely read daily newspaper.

Stilton was awarded the Ratitzer Prize for his scoops on *The Curse of the Cheese Pyramid* and *The Search for Sunken Treasure*. He has also received the Andersen 2000 Prize for Personality of the Year. One of his bestsellers won the 2002 eBook Award for world's best ratlings' electronic book. His works have been published all over the globe.

In his spare time, Mr. Stilton collects antique cheese rinds and plays golf. But what he most enjoys is telling stories to his nephew Benjamin.

1. Main entrance
2. Printing presses (where the books and newspaper are printed)
3. Accounts department
4. Editorial room (where the editors, illustrators, and designers work)
5. Geronimo Stilton's office
6. Helicopter landing pad

THE RODENT'S GAZETTE

Map of New Mouse City

Map of Mouse Island

1. Big Ice Lake
2. Frozen Fur Peak
3. Slipperyslopes Glacier
4. Coldcreeps Peak
5. Ratzikistan
6. Transratania
7. Mount Vamp
8. Roastedrat Volcano
9. Brimstone Lake
10. Poopedcat Pass
11. Stinko Peak
12. Dark Forest
13. Vain Vampires Valley
14. Goose Bumps Gorge
15. The Shadow Line Pass
16. Penny Pincher Castle
17. Nature Reserve Park
18. Las Ratayas Marinas
19. Fossil Forest
20. Lake Lake

21. Lake Lakelake
22. Lake Lakelakelake
23. Cheddar Crag
24. Cannycat Castle
25. Valley of the Giant Sequoia
26. Cheddar Springs
27. Sulfurous Swamp
28. Old Reliable Geyser
29. Vole Vale
30. Ravingrat Ravine
31. Gnat Marshes
32. Munster Highlands
33. Mousehara Desert
34. Oasis of the Sweaty Camel
35. Cabbagehead Hill
36. Rattytrap Jungle
37. Rio Mosquito

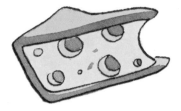

Dear mouse friends,
Thanks for reading, and farewell
till the next book.
It'll be another whisker-licking-good
adventure, and that's a promise!

Geronimo Stilton